# My Clothes

Illustrated by Fraser Williamson

Rigby

my socks

my boots

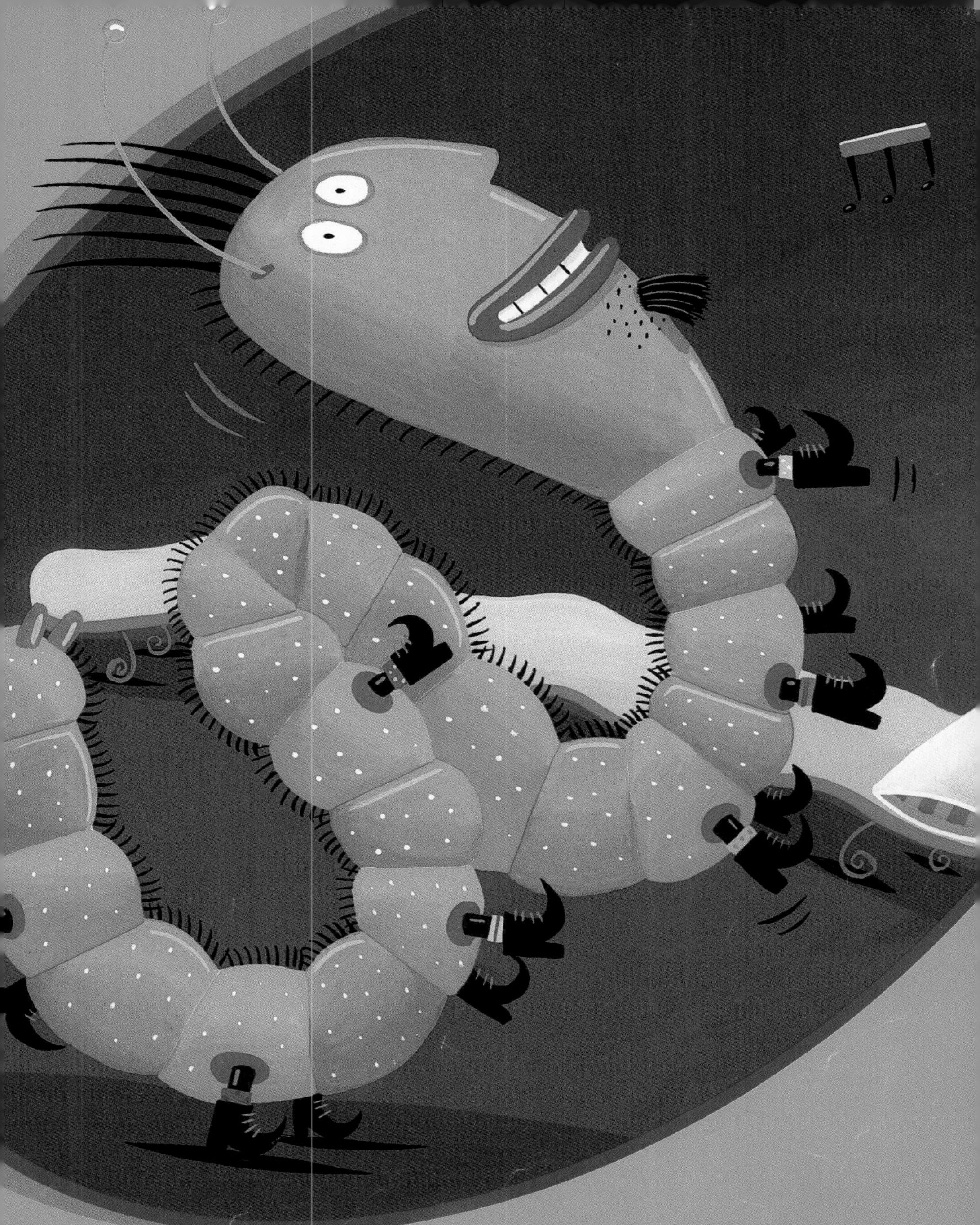

my tie

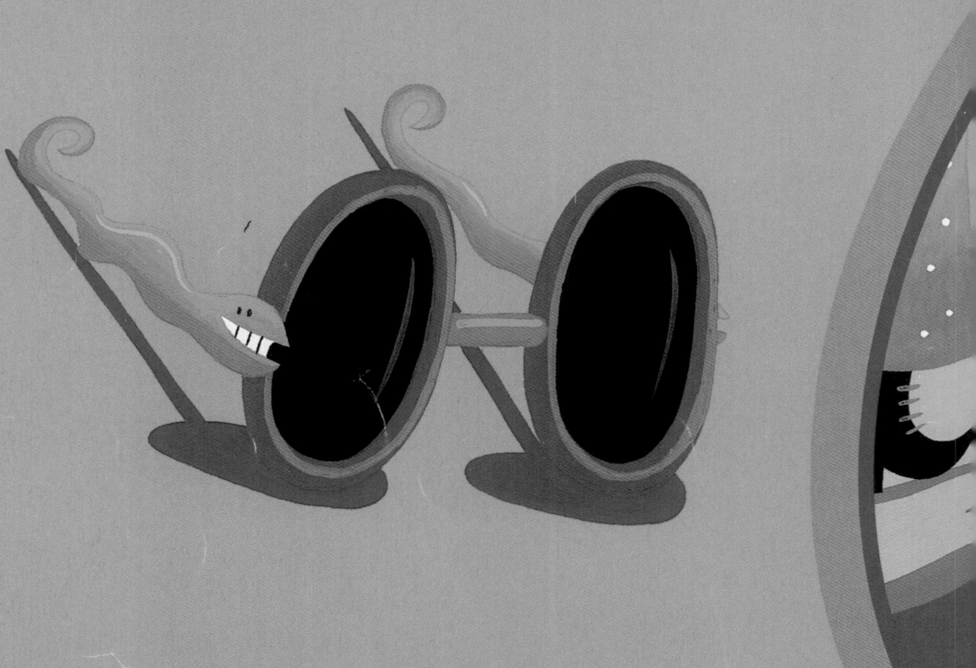

my glasses

my hat

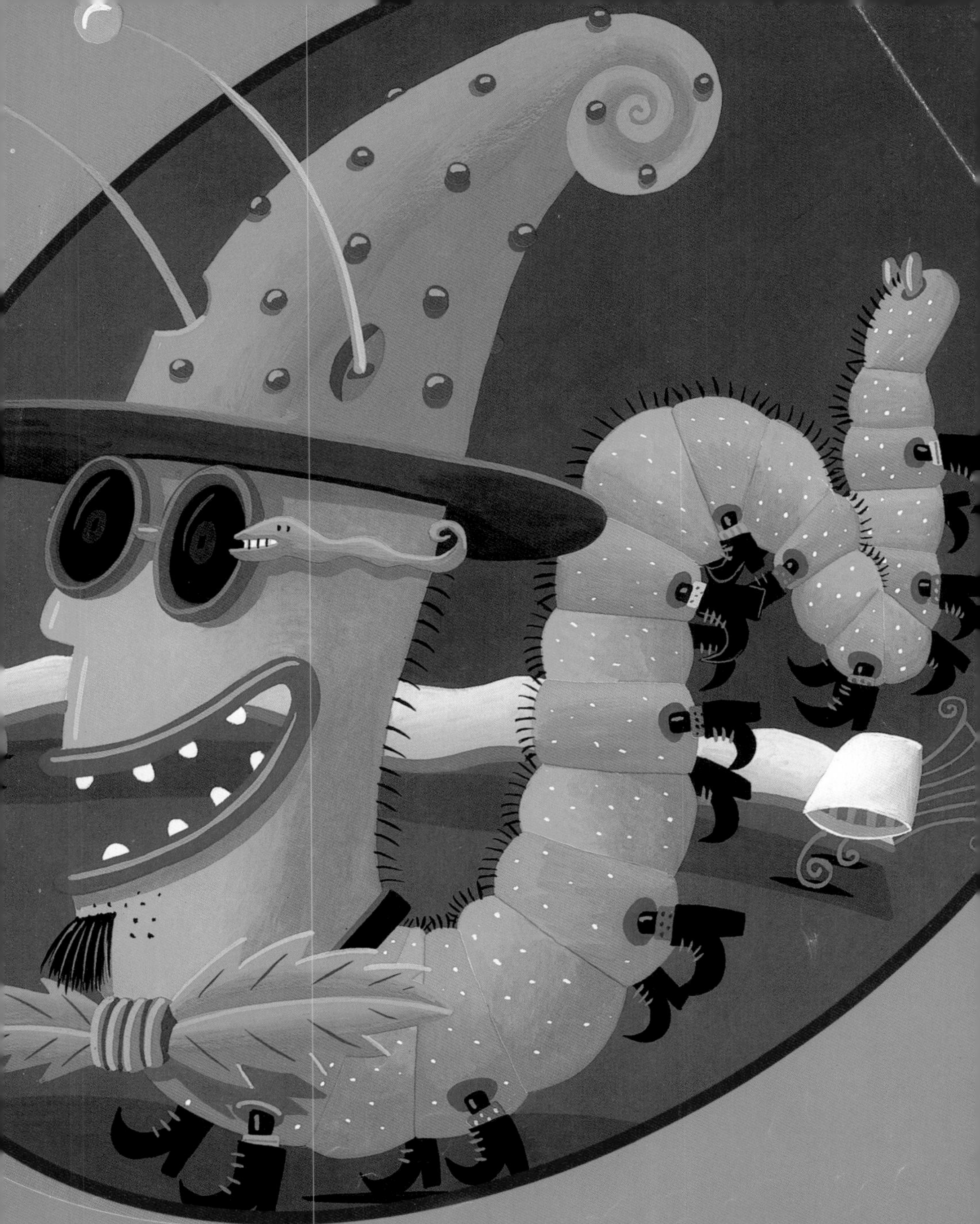

my belt

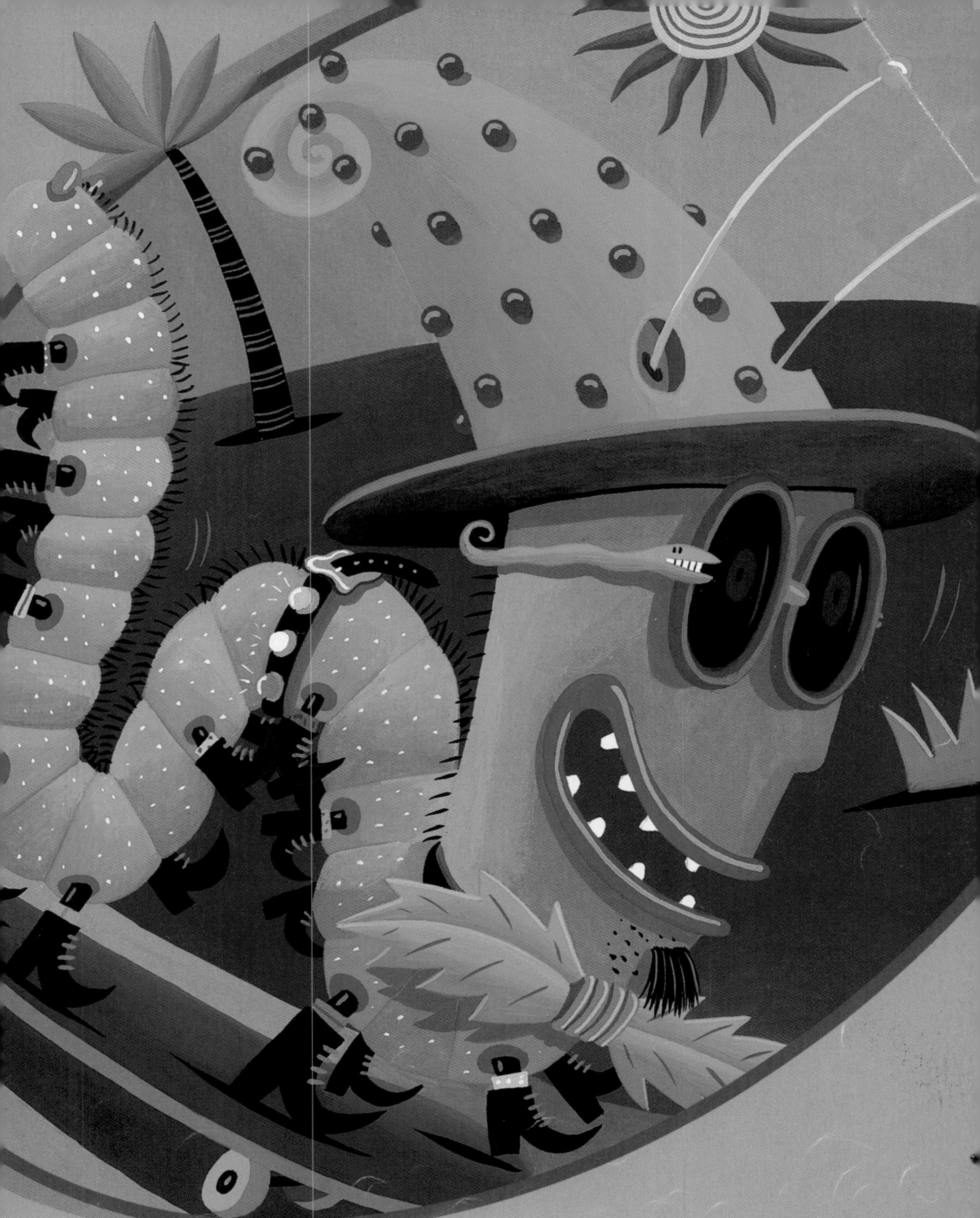

My sock!

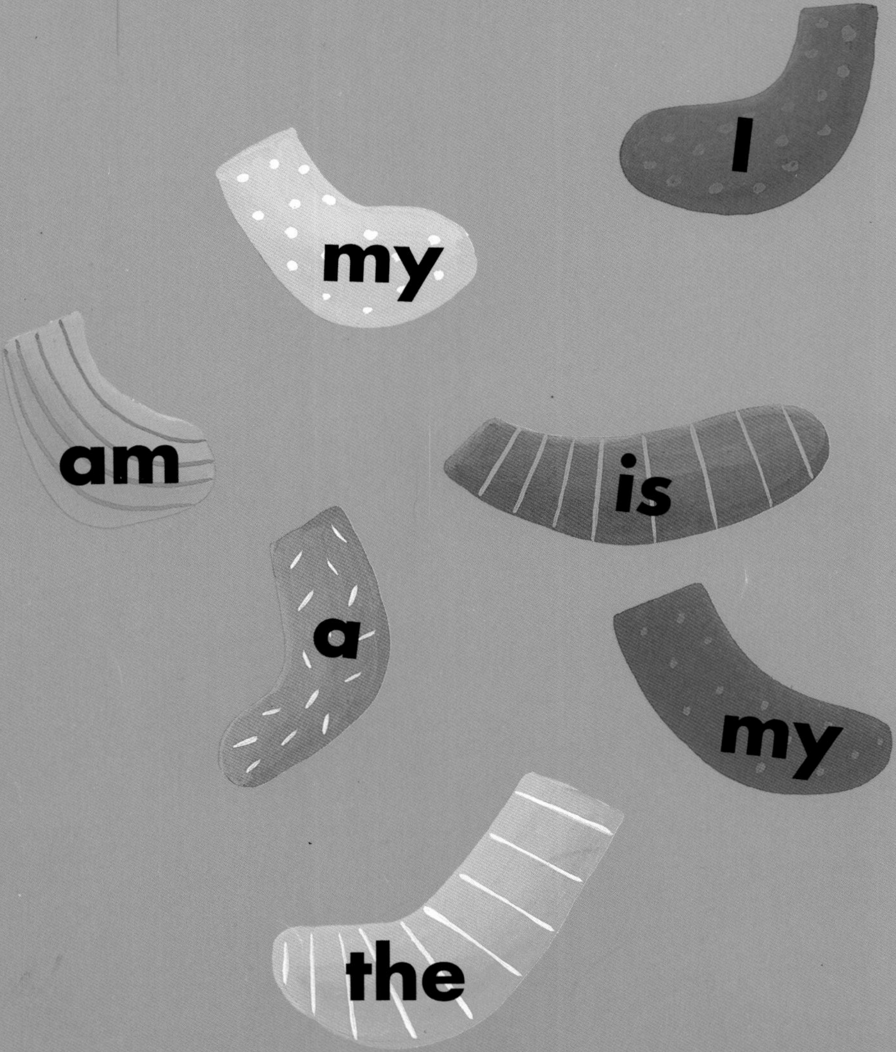
I
my
am
is
a
my
the